TEENEAGRAM

TEENEAGRAM

Identity Search Made Easy

Randy Winston Hillier

Library of Congress Control Number:		2016912497
ISBN:	Hardcover	978-1-5245-2942-0
	Softcover	978-1-5245-2941-3
	eBook	978-1-5245-2940-6

Rev. date: 09/28/2016

To order additional copies of this book, contact:
Xlibris
1-888-795-4274
www.Xlibris.com
Orders@Xlibris.com
735228

CONTENTS

Certificate of Registration

This Certificate issued under the seal of the Copyright
Office in accordance with title 17, *United States Code*,
attests that registration has been made for the work
identified below. The information on this certificate has
been made a part of the Copyright Office records.

Maria A. Pallante

Register of Copyrights, United States of America

Registration Number

TXu 1-923-968

Effective Date of Registration:
April 28, 2014

Title

Title of Work: "Teeneagram Identity Search Made Easy"

Completion/Publication

Year of Completion: 2014

Author

- **Author:** Randy Winston Hillier
  Author Created: a book that describes a personality system for adolescents
  Work made for hire: No
  Citizen of: United States
  Year Born: 1950
  Anonymous: No
  Pseudonymous: No

- **Author:** Gina Brostmeyer
  Author Created: illustrator
  Work made for hire: No
  Citizen of: United States
  Year Born: 1957

Copyright Claimant

Copyright Claimant: Randy Winston Hillier
1106 W. 36th St., San Pedro, CA, 90731

Limitation of copyright claim

Previously registered: No

Certification

Name: Randy Winston Hillier
Date: April 20, 2014

Dedicated to:
my son Aaron,
who always challenged me
to find a better way.
And to Robin who was
always by my side.

Acknowledgements

This book is a result of many helpful hands. I am foremost indebted to my adolescent/ young adult patients, who in their developing interest of the Enneagram, supported me in writing a book that would target a younger audience. I am deeply appreciative of the creative work of Gina Brostmeyer in developing the original illustrations and to my sister, Leslie Winston who devoted endless hours editing the material up until the book went to press.

I want to thank family, friends, and colleagues for their encouragement and ongoing support and feedback. To my original teachers and mentors, Helen Palmer and David Daniels, who introduced me to this work in 1986.

And lastly, I want to extend my appreciation to my amazing team at Xlibris Publishers who have provided me with a professional, generous, and cooperative working relationship over this past year.

PREFACE

I'm not strange, weird off, nor crazy,
my reality is just different than yours.
—Lewis Carroll

Adolescence offers a world mixed with excitement, challenge, and wonder. As you begin the daunting task of understanding yourself, you will experience periods during which you are likely to feel misunderstood, lonely, and self-conscious.

As I prepared myself to write these pages, I took the opportunity to reread my journals and poetry from my teen and young adult years. What struck me as interesting was how *familiar* I appeared to myself after all this time. I recognized in my writing that I was querulous and curious, dramatic and chaotic, and intense and moody. Now forty-five years later, what I am today is actually not that different from who I was back then. *The primary difference is how I manage and deal with myself and my reactions.* I hardly knew as a teen the many aspects of my identity and how they would one day become integrated.

My "search for identity" has been an ongoing quest. I took the career track of becoming a psychotherapist, so I immersed myself in the study of self, interpersonal relationships, communication, and all the other intriguing material offered at that time. I also had some basic understanding of meditation and what was called self-observation practices. Today it is referred to as mindfulness practice.

In my study over the years, I had some idea that personality can and does mask the "real self," and many books discussed the importance of becoming one's own actualized person. Secretly, I never fully understood what the authors were talking about. There were many descriptions about "false personality" and theories on how to develop one's authentic self. Yet I never found that the readings completely addressed what was going on inside of me. *The worries, preoccupations, and habits stayed basically the same, even if the objects of my attention changed.* I always suffered in similar ways. It was a painful, repetitive cycle.

"Would you tell me please, which way I ought to go from here?"
"That depends a good deal on where you want to get to," said the Cat.
"I don't much care where," said Alice.

"Then it doesn't matter which way you go," said the Cat.
"So long as I get somewhere," Alice added as an explanation.
"Oh, you're sure to do that," said the Cat, "if you only walk enough."
—*Lewis Carroll*

When I discovered the Enneagram, now written for teens as *Teeneagram*, I realized that I had discovered an amazing road map that would offer me a way to understand my developing self and identity. I am forever grateful to having learned this powerful system as a way of seeing and paying attention to myself and others.

INTRODUCTION

But if I'm not the same, the question is,
"Who in the world am I?"
Ah, that's the great puzzle!
— *Lewis Carroll*

The *Teeneagram* is an "internal operating system" and will help you navigate your way in the world. Since your OS (operating system) is the basic structure that supports your personality type, you will learn that your inner life is fully connected to how you live, interact, communicate, and behave in the world.

"Who are you?" said the Caterpillar.
This was not an encouraging opening for a conversation.
Alice replied, rather shyly, "I-I hardly know, sir, just at present—at least
I know who I was when I got up this morning, but I think I must have
changed several times since then."
— *Lewis Carroll*

Had Alice known the *Teeneagram*, she would have learned that since attention does shift, that one does alter at particular times. However, how one shifts is specific to each *Teeneagram* point. The movement follows a pattern that is built into the system. The *Teeneagram* offers us a tool to observe ourselves and specifically teaches us what we need to pay attention to in order to grow. Since we all struggle with aspects of ourselves, it helps identify our style of attention in order to make the necessary changes to overcome our unhappiness and pain. The steps are as follows: spend time inside yourself and use the *Teeneagram* as your road map, identify your *Teeneatype* point, and observe over time how this type plays out in your life. As you use the system, you will begin to identify patterns and habits that offer you additional insight into your inner self and the reasons you react the way you do.

"Where shall I begin, please, Your Majesty?" he asked.
"Begin at the beginning," the king said gravely,
"and go on till you come to the end then stop."
— *Lewis Carroll*

I remain enthusiastic and optimistic that each of you, who are interested in understanding yourselves and even others, will benefit from learning the *Teeneagram*. I have attempted to both condense and simplify the material as much as possible without detracting from the richness of the information and its sources. The path of self-awareness is a true gift.

> *But said Alice, "The world has absolutely no sense.*
> *Who's stopping us from inventing one?"*
>
> *—Lewis Carroll*

What Is the Enneagram?

Imagine, if you can, that you, like Alice, have fallen down the rabbit hole. Now nothing makes much sense, and you feel misunderstood and confused much of the time. The rabbit hole starts the journey to help you understand just how you can transform. It is only when Alice comes out the other end of the rabbit hole that she begins to have many amazing experiences. In the story, Alice changes her size twelve times. At first, Alice is trying to make sense of the world, and it appears that no one is particularly concerned by Alice's confusion. Over time, however, things begin to happen.

> *The Caterpillar was the first to speak.*
> *"What size do you want to be?" it asked.*
> *"Oh, I'm not particular to size," Alice hastily replied.*
> *"Only one doesn't like changing so often, you know."*
> *"I don't know," said the Caterpillar.*
> *Alice said nothing. She had never been so much*
> *contradicted in all her life before, and she felt that*
> *she was losing her temper.*

Again, if Alice had understood the Enneagram, now named *Teeneagram*, she would have known there was a psychological chart made of nine points each of which represents a particular point from which we view the world, understand people, and think about ourselves. Alice, like you, also needs to understand that these different points of view come about because people pay attention in different ways to different things.

At the Mad Tea Party, Alice was considered a party crasher.

> *The table was a large one, but the three were all crowded together at one corner of it.*
> "No room! No room!" *they cried out when they saw Alice coming.*
> "There's plenty of room," *said Alice indignantly, and she sat down in a large arm chair at the end of the table.*

It's hard to know what Alice was paying attention to initially, but it was most likely different from the preoccupations of the March Hare, Mad Hatter, and Dormouse. Alice was most likely thinking about herself with no idea that she might be interrupting a private conversation.

The reason you and Alice need to understand how attention works is to discover how it is organized in very specific ways and can be changed. It is important to realize that our inner thoughts, feelings, and behaviors are very helpful if we can recognize our patterns and what triggers them. When we don't understand ourselves, particularly when we are suffering, we don't always know what to do.

> *The last time she saw them, they were trying to put Dormouse into the teapot.*
>
> *"At any rate, I'll never go there again!" said Alice as she picked her way through the wood. "It's the stupidest tea party I ever was at in my life!"*

Our personality is composed of the thoughts, feelings, and behaviors that are unique to our individual selves. In contrast, our attention requires us to develop a keen self-observer and a place to go within ourselves where we can actually shut off our personality. When we are able to do that, we can shift our focus at will and overcome our pain and suffering.

The major task during adolescence is to figure out who you are and the direction you want to grow. Much of the turmoil that occurs at this time is a result of physical, mental, and emotional changes that are outside of your control.

> *"Well, perhaps you haven't found it so yet," said Alice, "but when you have to turn into a chrysalis—you will someday, you know—and then after that into a butterfly, I should think you'll feel it a little queer, won't you?"*
>
> *"Not a bit," said the Caterpillar.*
>
> *"Well, perhaps your feelings may be different," said Alice. "All I know is it would feel very queer to me."*
>
> *"You," said the Caterpillar contemptuously. "Who are you?"*

Much of your social life is based on figuring out who the people are that are like you versus those who are different from you. This is a time when you might change your friends a lot. All these relationships help you figure out who you will eventually become. You are also experimenting with your ability to distance yourself from your parents and become your own person. You might even have noticed the different ways your friends talk and act toward their parents.

If you recognize that during adolescence, you have many opportunities to grow and change; think of all the better choices you can make if you understand the habits, patterns, and ideas that already exist inside of you and how they are organized. This will enable you to choose positive behaviors and make informed decisions that meet both your needs and your goals.

THE ENNEAGRAM CHART

Direct your attention to the image on this page, and you will see a circle with an inner triangle. Six additional points form a zigzag pattern, both cutting though the inner triangle and then finding a numerical point along the circle.

The inner triangle points 9, 6, and 3 are called anger, fear, and image points respectively. The other remaining six points are variations of these particular points.

THE WINGS OF EACH "TEENEATYPE" POINT

The wings are the points that are directly to the left and right of each *Teeneatype* point. For example, point three has wings of points two and four. The personality of a twoish-three will be quite different from a fourish-three. The wings of each *Teeneatype* will be discussed along with each character.

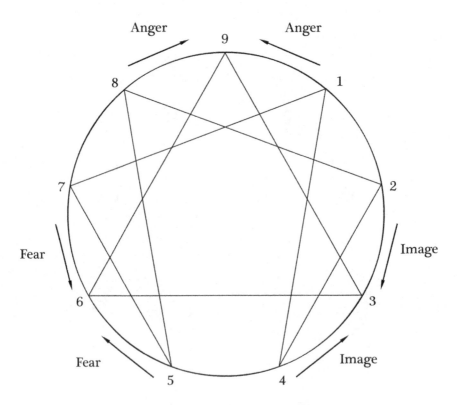

ALICE COMES ABOARD

"My name is Alice, so please, Your Majesty," said Alice very politely; but she added, to herself, "Why, they're only a pack of cards, after all, I need not be afraid of them!"

Alice has finally relented and decided to learn the Teeneagram. She has invited you to join her on her new adventure. On the remaining pages of this chapter, you will find a set of true and false cards followed by a set of cards with checklists on the bottom half of each page. To play the card game, cut out the fifty-four cards. Then shuffle them and place them in a stack. Now answer the questions and place the cards that you answered true in piles that represent each of the Teeneatypes. Whenever you accumulate three cards of the same type, refer to the Teeneatype cards with checklists to see if you mostly agree with the card's character traits. You will most likely identify your Teeneatype through a process of elimination.

As you read further, each chapter will provide you with additional information to help you identify your type and see how your "distant cousins" are both like you and different from you.

I can't go back to yesterday because I was a different person then.

I have an inner critic that always tells me what I am doing, both right and wrong. It's a black and white thing; there is nothing in between.

If true place in a pile for Peggy.

I have a lot of "shoulds," such as "I should do my homework," "I should study for my test," and "I should keep up with my daily responsibilities." I feel guilty if I don't follow through.

If true place in a pile for Peggy.

I focus on self-improvement and believe effort "should" be rewarded. I try to be the best I can and follow all the rules.

If true place in a pile for Peggy.

I get resentful when others get by with things they shouldn't.

If true place in a pile for Peggy.

I strive for perfection. I work hard to get A's and will work for extra credit if that is what it takes.

If true place in a pile for Peggy.

I make lists to help me get things done. My friends count on me to have the correct assignments written down.

If true place in a pile for Peggy.

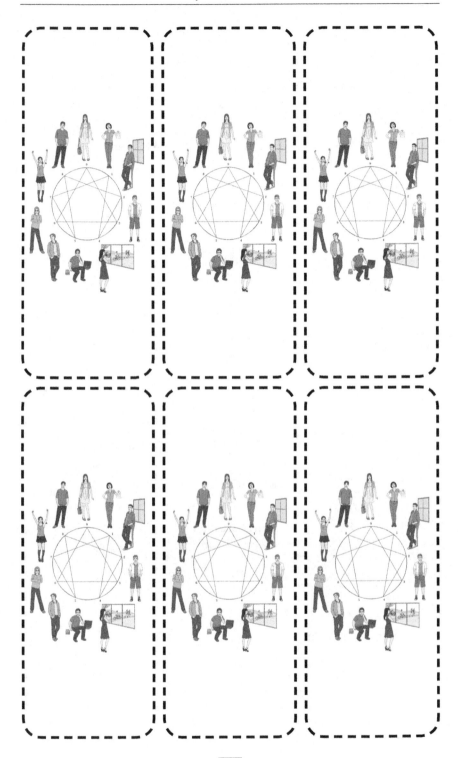

I don't always know what I need for myself. I am so busy taking care of everyone else both at home and at school.

If true place in a pile for Franklin.

My friends often come to me with their problems. They count on me to be available and give them good advice.

If true place in a pile for Franklin.

I feel best about myself when others appreciate my help. Approval is important to me.

If true place in a pile for Franklin.

I feel good about myself when others ask me for my help at school.

If true place in a pile for Franklin.

I will go out of my way to be helpful. Approval is important to me.

If true place in a pile for Franklin.

I find that I act differently around various friends. I do it mostly to make them feel comfortable.

If true place in a pile for Franklin.

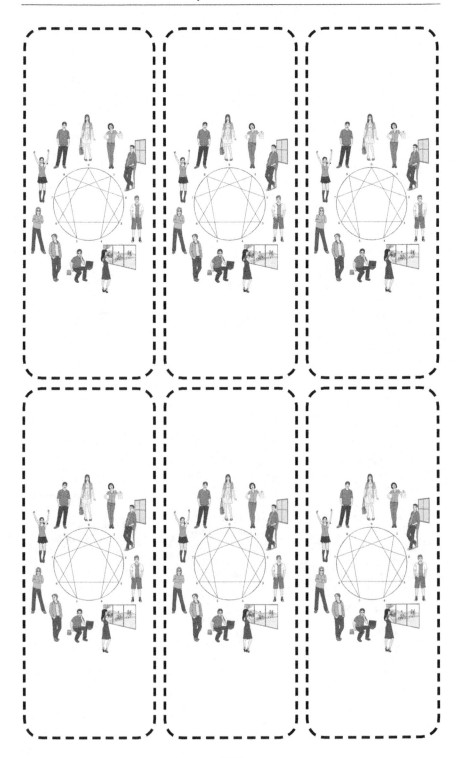

I want to be popular, get good grades, and excel in school and community activities.

If true place in a pile for Trent.

I already have a lot of goals for my future. I think about college and career choices. I want to be very successful.

If true place in a pile for Trent.

I have a packed schedule. I am always doing something to meet my goals.

If true place in a pile for Trent.

When I am with my friends we are always doing something. I don't like to just sit around and hang out. I find that boring.

If true place in a pile for Trent.

I am usually not aware of my feelings. I find that they can get in the way of everything I have to do.

If true place in a pile for Trent.

I always know how to act in every situation. I can easily adapt to playing the role of student, athlete, friend, etc. They are all part of who I am.

If true place in a pile for Trent.

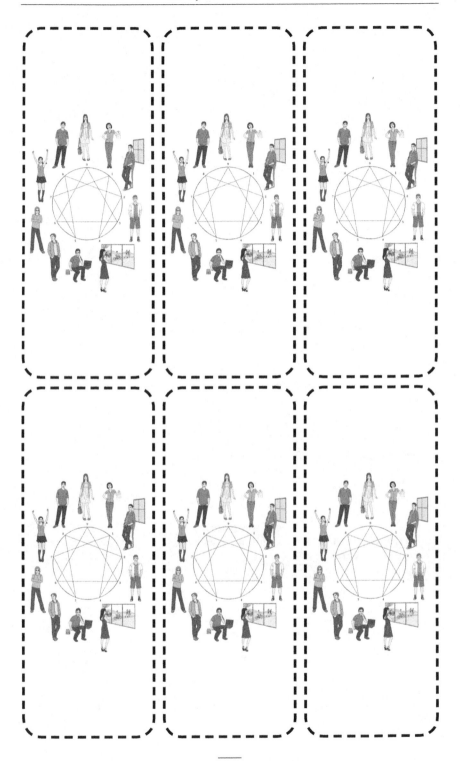

I believe that I am missing out on things. It often feels that more interesting things are going on somewhere else.

If true place in a pile for Maria.

I am easily hurt and can feel abandoned if a friend forgets to call me.

If true place in a pile for Maria.

I seem to feel things more deeply than my friends or other people I know.

If true place in a pile for Maria.

I like to be unique and tend to create my own artistic style.

If true place in a pile for Maria.

I tend to be dramatic, and I am often misunderstood. My friends even tell me that I am too sensitive.

If true place in a pile for Maria.

My creativity matters a great deal. I use art, music, poetry, and fashion to express my personal style.

If true place in a pile for Maria.

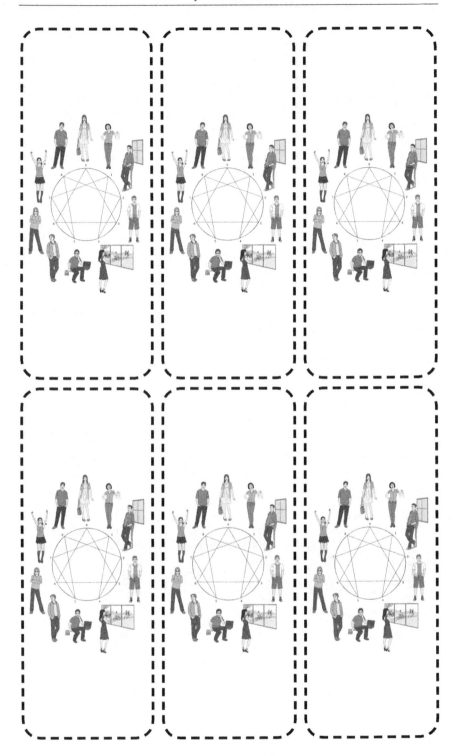

It happens that I have different friends who don't know one another. I like to keep parts of my life separate.

If true place in a pile for Mark.

When I notice that my bedroom is a mess, I wish I had a system to keep it all organized.

If true place in a pile for Mark.

I like my privacy. My parents always think I am being secretive or hiding something.

If true place in a pile for Mark.

Feelings are not easy for me to figure out immediately. I like to review them after an experience when I am by myself.

If true place in a pile for Mark.

I am always observing and thinking about things. Others think I am preoccupied and that I live in my head.

If true place in a pile for Mark.

My friends think I am really smart. They count on me to help them with research projects and classes that require problem solving.

If true place in a pile for Mark.

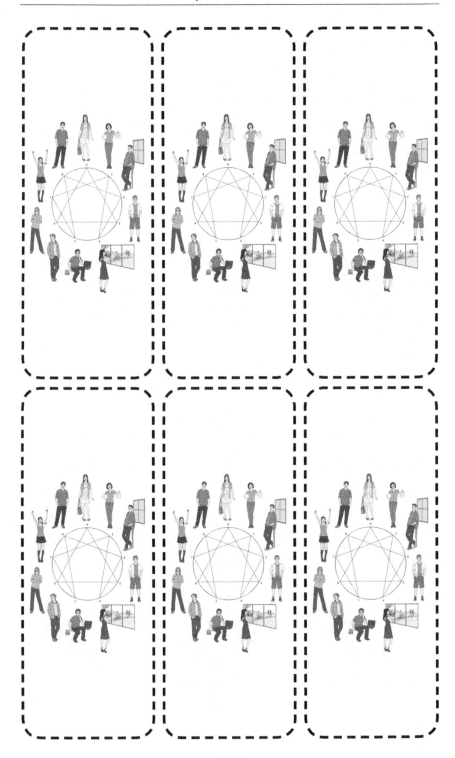

I often distrust authority. I hate being told what to do. I often tune out my parents and teachers if they are telling me to do something I don't want to do.

If true place in a pile for Paul and Rusty.

I get a thrill from taking risks, challenges, and being in dangerous situations.

If true place in a pile for Paul and Rusty.

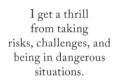

I can overthink things. "I wonder why that older girl is smiling at me?" "Why is that kid standing near my locker?"

If true place in a pile for Paul and Rusty.

I tend to have a lot of self-doubt. "Did I study enough?" "Is my friend mad at me?" "Did I remember to turn in my homework?"

If true place in a pile for Paul and Rusty.

It's hard to trust even my friends. I always try to figure out other people's motives. Who is loyal, and who might betray me?

If true place in a pile for Paul and Rusty.

Sometimes my fears seem so real I freak myself out.

If true place in a pile for Paul and Rusty.

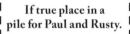

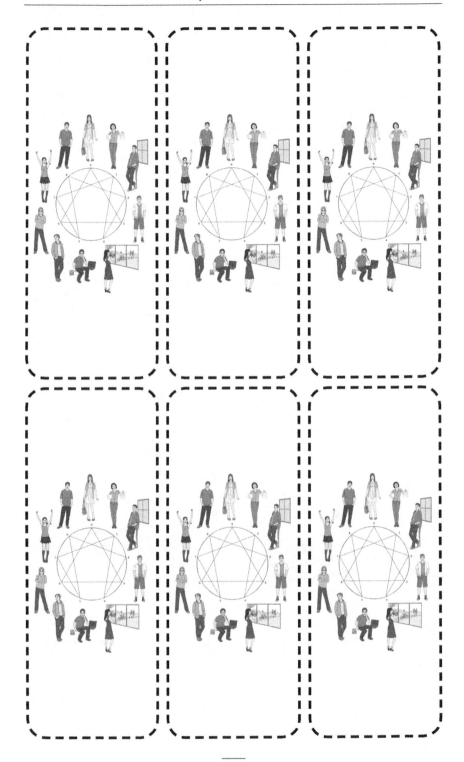

As soon as someone wants a commitment from me, I feel like things are closing in on me. I always like to have an out or another option available.

If true place in a pile for Penny.

My mind is usually going a mile a minute. I can easily get caught up in fantasizing and planning new experiences.

If true place in a pile for Penny.

I like to keep things light and fun. Friends who complain and talk about their problems don't hold my interest.

If true place in a pile for Penny.

I can be really focused on something. Then something else catches my attention, and I move my attention there. I am known to change topics in a conversation all the time.

If true place in a pile for Penny.

I am upbeat and positive, so people are always attracted to me.

If true place in a pile for Penny.

I don't like being pinned down, and I like to keep my options open. I usually make a lot of plans for the weekend, and then when the time comes, I decide what to do at the last minute.

If true place in a pile for Penny.

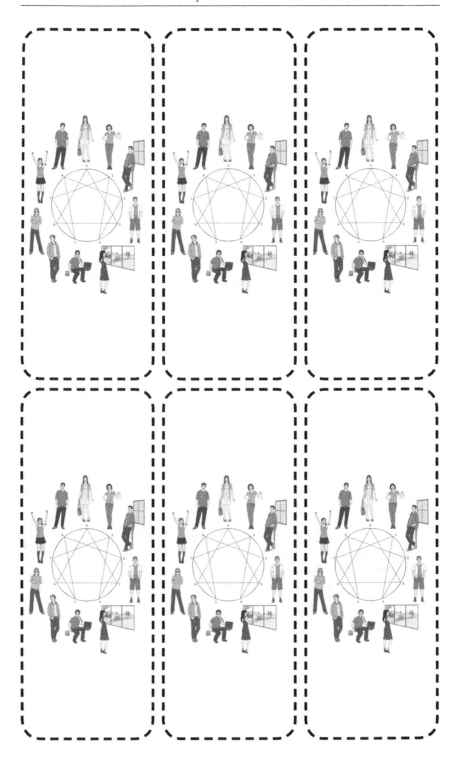

I am competitive with myself and others. I have a large committee in my head that is usually arguing about something.

If true place in a pile for Conrad.

I am protective of the weak and helpless. Whether it's a little kid crying, a stray dog, or a homeless person, my heart goes out to them.

If true place in a pile for Conrad.

When I feel like crying or when my sensitive side shows, I see it as a weakness. I would rather be seen as tough.

If true place in a pile for Conrad.

My anger is always bubbling to the surface, especially if I see or experience an injustice.

If true place in a pile for Conrad.

I get in trouble for speaking the truth and then told I am out of line.

If true place in a pile for Conrad.

My friends tell me I am often bossy and controlling, but I just take charge. Otherwise, nothing happens.

If true place in a pile for Conrad.

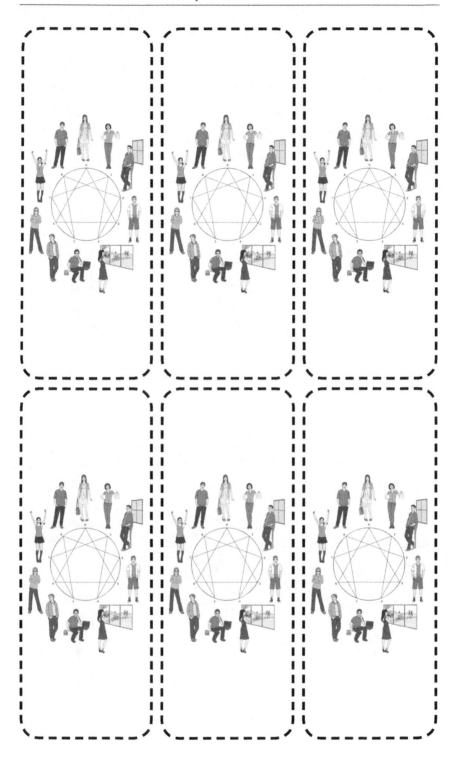

Because I mostly understand everyone else, it is easy for my friends to come talk to me. They often want my advice.

If true place in a pile for Sarah.

I can get stuck in my own distractions. I can sit down to play a video game or go on the computer, and before I know it, three hours have passed.

If true place in a pile for Sarah.

It is just easier to go along with people. I dislike conflict and avoid it at all costs.

If true place in a pile for Sarah.

Only some things are important to me. Many times I can't seem to stay motivated and easily run out of steam.

If true place in a pile for Sarah.

I get in trouble for procrastinating. Sometimes, even when I finished my homework, I forget to turn it in.

If true place in a pile for Sarah.

It is hard for me to hold a position. As soon as I hear others opinions I can be persuaded to change my mind.

If true place in a pile for Sarah.

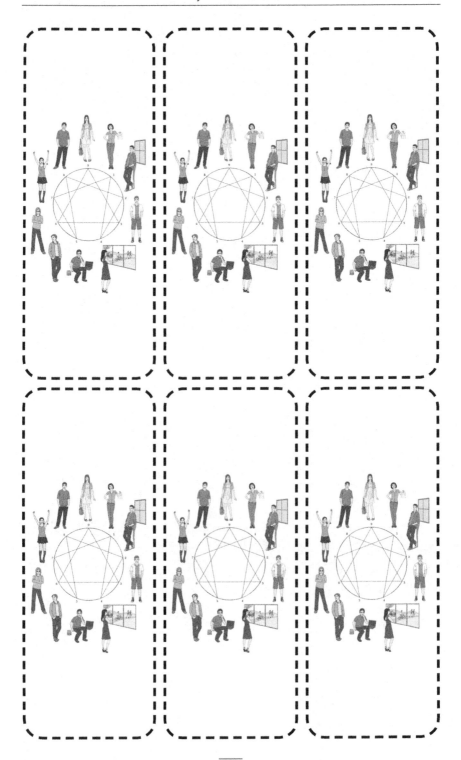

Conrad the Challenger	Sarah the Mediator	Peggy the Perfectionist

Point 8	Point 9	Point 1

BODY TYPES

Bossy ☐	Avoids Conflict ☐	Has a lot of shoulds and a sense of correctness ☐
Challenging and controlling ☐	Sees everyone's point of view, just not her own ☐	Her inner critic runs overtime ☐
Protective ☐	Trouble being self-motivated, accused of being lazy ☐	Can be judgmental and critical ☐
Can be oppositional ☐	Doesn't like change ☐	Rigid and rule-oriented ☐
Difficulty managing anger ☐	Gets stuck in inertia and spacing out ☐	Focus on self-improvement ☐
Big energy "nothing too much" ☐	Trouble expressing needs ☐	Trouble taking criticism ☐
Competitive ☐	Can be passive-aggressive ☐	Can have a good sense of humor ☐
Seeks the truth ☐	Goes with the flow ☐	Strives for perfection ☐
Sees vulnerability as weakness ☐	When angry takes a long time to get over it ☐	Doing it right the first time ☐
Impulsive and lustful ☐	Procrastinates ☐	Makes a lot of lists to get things done ☐

Franklin the Giver	Trent the Performer	Maria the Tragic Romantic

Point 2	Point 3	Point 4

HEART TYPES

Prideful ☐	High achiever ☐	Needs to be unique and special ☐
Seeks approval ☐	Performance replaces feelings ☐	Creativity is important ☐
Feels good about self by giving ☐	Not aware of feelings ☐	Feelings of envy "the grass is always greener on the other side" ☐
Flatters others ☐	Goals and tasks take priority ☐	Moody and melancholy ☐
Identity changes to others' liking ☐	Self-image based on getting things done ☐	Does push-pull in relationships ☐
Codependent ☐	Image is important ☐	Seeks to be authentic and deep ☐
Trouble knowing needs ☐	Can play different roles comfortably ☐	Self-critical ☐
Sensitive to others ☐	Focus on success and ambition ☐	Idealized view of self and others ☐
Self-image based on others' opinions ☐	Can develop self-doubt ☐	Issues of abandonment push-pull ☐
Anger can be explosive ☐	Always scheduled ☐	Sensitive and empathetic ☐

Mark the Observer	Paul and Rusty the Troopers	Penny the Optimist

Point 5	Point 6	Point 7

HEAD TYPES

Likes his privacy	☐	Very fearful	☐	Optimistic	☐
Observes others	☐	Challenges and attacks fear head-on	☐	Upbeat and positive	☐
Collects knowledge	☐	Loyal	☐	Trouble with commitment	☐
Tends to minimize	☐	Takes on underdog causes	☐	Keeps options open	☐
Natural detective	☐	Anti-authority	☐	High levels of stimulation	☐
Likes to analyze and problem solve	☐	Likes problem solving	☐	Focused then easily distracted	☐
Reviews feelings in private	☐	Has a lot of self-doubt	☐	Keeps things light	☐
Lives in his head	☐	Difficulty trusting others	☐	Can be critical	☐
Compartmentalizes by keeping his life in separate boxes	☐	Overthinks things	☐	Wants a lot of experiences	☐
Doesn't express feelings easily	☐	Detail-minded	☐	Avoids anything negative	☐

Peggy the Perfectionist

Point 1

Let's meet Peggy.

From the outside:

Peggy is quite impressive. We can associate her capital P for Peggy with words such as *perfectionistic, punctual, poised, polite, proper, and parental.* When others see Peggy, she appears to have it all together. She usually gets her homework done before everyone else. She makes time for hobbies, volunteer work, helping her mom out, and extra reading and is still available for friends. She is easily the "teacher's pet."

Peggy is the classic "all-American Girl" and almost a little old-fashioned in another respect. Even so, it is hard not to like Peggy because she is so nice and innocent-looking, always doing the right thing and is so purr-fect it is kind of sickly sweet.

Peggy can get annoying when she becomes critical and judgmental. When Peggy is uptight, her body looks tense and rigid. Peggy can appear really angry and not even know it. When she gets mean and irritated, it is because she believes she is right about everything. It can sound like she is giving a lecture. Who does she think she is—my mother?

What is going on inside of Peggy?

What could be Peggy's serenity and peace of mind has been replaced by a voice inside her head, an *inner critic*. "Shoulds" have come to replace her needs. This voice always tells Peggy what to improve on or what to do differently. The *inner critic* behaves like a boss. Ideals, principles, and standards are expected to be met. When they aren't met, the *inner critic* will tend to scold her, and all attention is focused on getting Peggy back in line. Needs that operate as the adult voice, which offers objective information regarding what one requires, have been overruled by the inner parent. Peggy is also afraid that if she stops doing what she is supposed to do, something bad will happen.

Peggy's inner world is black and white. She can easily experience anxiety and anger since she needs her life to be a certain way, a way that allows for routine, structure, and regularity. It is only when she follows her rules that she feels that she has earned time off and can reward herself with rest and relaxation.

MOVEMENT IN THE ENNEAGRAM

In the Enneagram system, you move directly to two other points, in addition to the wings. This can vary from situation to situation. For point one, the movement is to point four and point seven.

When Peggy moves to four:

When Peggy's attention moves to four, her inner focus and behaviors look more like the "tragic-romantic" point. On the positive side, she can be creative and artistic and explore the deeper meaning of life. But more than likely Peggy experiences four when she is sad and lonely or feeling misunderstood. She feels a sense of having "messed up" in a big way. In four, Peggy can break her own rules, escape into fantasy, or become moody and withdrawn.

Peggy feels no one understands how hard she truly works and thinks others are judging and disapproving of her. Most of these thoughts are created by her *inner critic*. Now her sense of guilt is replaced by feeling sorry for herself and taking on the role of victim.

When Peggy moves to seven:

There are times when Peggy moves to point seven. Here, the inner critic takes a break and Peggy can relax into a more spontaneous and optimistic view of life. She can take pleasure in exploring options and fun activities. The reins of maintaining self-control are loosened. It is a relief for Peggy to be less rigid and controlled. But she has to be careful, however, to monitor herself, or she might put on hold the things she needs to do. Sometimes, in seven, she forgets entirely about a specific responsibility or "should." In seven, Peggy can daydream and fantasize about wonderful possibilities. For the moment, all practical, realistic considerations are forgotten. She relaxes, is positive, and enjoys life.

Peggy and Romantic Relationships:

Boyfriends are a mixed blessing for Peggy. Because she is "the all-American girl," boys are attracted to her. What they don't know is that they will be on probation for quite some time. Peggy usually sees the new crush through rose-colored glasses (i.e., she sees the relationship as if it were completely wonderful). Then Peggy fantasizes and imagines how it is going to be.

The problem is that her expectations can be unrealistic because she has a set of standards and "shoulds" for both the boy and herself that are impossible to maintain. However, because Peggy has the rose-colored glasses on, along with her "shoulds," she can sometimes make excuses for "bad behavior" and when the relationship falls short of her expectations.

Without these excuses, Peggy could become critical and judgmental or easily hurt. It is like being on a seesaw, struggling for the balance of seeing the other person clearly and figuring out what one *should* do versus what one *should* expect from a relationship.

Peggy and Friendships:

Peggy has high standards for her friends. She knows how to get along with everyone because she knows the correct thing to do. The way Peggy shows she cares is in her attempts at improving her friends. Peggy readily volunteers her opinions and offers advice without being asked. She sees this as helpful and necessary in order to help improve her friends' lives. On the other hand, it is very difficult for Peggy to receive advice and take criticism because she feels that she is already trying so hard. When she is corrected, she feels like she has made some big mistake and feels hurt and upset with herself.

Peggy is true to her word, punctual, and dependable. When others mistreat her, she is offended and might decide she is done with that person. Friendships are taken seriously. Peggy is a loyal friend, but she will not compromise her principles. Don't ask Peggy to cover for you or break her own rules.

Case Vignette:

Peggy (point one) calls up Sarah (point nine) to suggest what Sarah should wear to the school dance. Peggy then tells Sarah that her hair could use a trim and new style and gives her the name of her salon. Sarah, lost for words, meekly thanks Peggy. The next day Peggy can't understand why Sarah avoids her and eats lunch at a different table.

Wings of Point One:

The wings are the points that are to either side of each *Teeneatype* point. The wings reflect certain features that make the actual point more inclusive of other qualities.

Two Wing:

If Peggy has a two wing, she will have some of the characteristics of Franklin, who you will meet in the next chapter. She will seek approval by being helpful and offering free advice. Her desire is to improve you for your own good.

Nine Wing:

If Peggy has a nine wing, she will be more contained and passive like Sarah, who you will meet in chapter nine. Peggy will see the different points of view of any situation, which will enable her to be less judgmental. Peggy will be less strict about the shoulds and the rules and tend to give others the benefit of the doubt.

Franklin the Giver

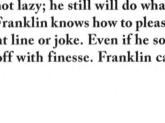

Point 2

Let's meet Franklin.

From the outside:

Franklin is quite the guy. His capital F for Franklin is associated with the words *friendly, forward, flirtatious, flighty,* and *flatterer.* Franklin is a lot like a "knight in shining armor." He knows how to be a gentleman and a good guy.

He always tends to others in a caring and a sensitive way. Franklin has the uncanny ability to tune into others' needs automatically. Because he is so accommodating and flexible, he is like a chameleon. He changes according to whom he is with. He can appear to be one way and then change his style and image to attune to someone else.

Franklin likes to be entertaining and prides himself on giving and going the extra step for people. Because he wants approval and needs to be liked, it is important to him to keep up appearances. Although Franklin can be manipulative, he is not lazy; he still will do whatever it takes to be esteemed and admired. Franklin knows how to please the girls and is always ready with the right line or joke. Even if he sounds a little phony, he manages to pull it off with finesse. Franklin can be charming, engaging, and witty.

What is going on inside of Franklin?

What could be Franklin's humility and self-acceptance is replaced by pride. Franklin has difficulty admitting his dependencies and has lost sight of his own needs. These have been replaced by a focus on meeting everyone else's needs. Franklin's identity is dependent on what others think of him. He requires constant approval, recognition, and reassurance to feel adequate.

Franklin gets particularly annoyed when he is referred to as Frank or Frankie. Franklin's self-importance requires a name that suits his image. Nicknames don't work. In Franklin's mind, he wants to appear mature and masculine. To be called Frank is bad enough, but Frankie feels like he is being addressed as a three-year-old.

Franklin seeks connection. He scans faces, particularly locking eyes with others to ensure connection. He mentally locks on to the thought *Does he or she like me?* The compulsive habit is to find ways to please the other. Franklin engages by using flattery. He smiles and flirts to get others to like him and give him attention. He tries to maintain a positive attitude in order to be agreeable and upbeat.

Although Franklin tries to be a good student, his attention is more focused on being involved in the lives of others. He solves their problems and offers them his help and his time. This leaves little time for him to take care of his own responsibilities and workload.

Franklin's focus of attention is external, so he loses sight of his inner self. Because he has trouble staying inner-directed, he easily becomes scattered and forgetful. It is difficult for Franklin to stay on track and to remain clear as to how he can best meet his own needs.

MOVEMENT IN THE ENNEAGRAM

In the Enneagram system, you move directly to two other points, in addition to the wings. This can vary from situation to situation. For point two, the movement is to point four and point eight.

When Franklin moves to four:

When Franklin moves to point four, he takes on the qualities of the tragic-romantic which helps shift his attention inward. This offers Franklin an opportunity to be more authentic and depth-oriented. Here, Franklin can get more in touch with his personal needs and have a fuller understanding of his more authentic self, since there is less need for approval and pleasing others. In point four, it is not just a sense of pride that causes him to want to be called Franklin rather than Frankie but also an inner identification of how he needs to project his self-image for himself.

In point four, Franklin, like Peggy, can feel misunderstood and experience hurt and sad feelings. In point four, Franklin can see how his codependent behaviors and giving is also a form of manipulation.

The more positive side of four enables Franklin to express his creative, artistic side. If he can balance his outward focus with more self-awareness, he will feel less empty and needy.

When Franklin moves to eight:

When Franklin is in point eight, no one will think of him as "Frankie." In point eight, Franklin demonstrates two very distinct positions. In eight, he can take charge and be extremely pushy and aggressive. He shows anger in an explosive way which is a result of feeling resentful that his own needs are not being met and that his efforts are not recognized. Giving and giving to the bare-bones, Franklin feels both empty and unappreciated, but instead of experiencing self-pity, he blames others and blasts his anger.

A more positive aspect of point eight is when Franklin becomes the protector and asserter. Here, he operates at his best in crisis management and taking charge of emotional, high-drama situations.

Franklin and Romantic Relationships:

Franklin is the ideal date. Prince Charming himself might have been a point two. He can be flirty and forward and will go after what he wants. Because of his desire for approval, Franklin can be the amazing boyfriend. The problem is that he is also "Mr. Nice Guy." So for all you girls who like "the bad boy pattern," you won't get that from Franklin unless he is in eight. Franklin will go so far as to even do your homework for you, although it might not be 100 percent accurate the way it would be if Peggy the Perfectionist did it for you. On second thought, Peggy wouldn't do it for you. She would call that cheating, which is against her ethical standards.

Franklin has the habit of doing push-pull in romantic relationships like Maria the four does. Franklin can also become possessive and jealous. He can get insecure if he doesn't receive attention and gratitude in return for all his giving. His primary desire and goal is to please you.

Franklin and Friendships:

Franklin is a caring friend. This is when he is most often referred to as "Frankie," which he loathes. It makes him feel like he is three years old. Frankie, I mean Franklin, is always the one everyone calls when they need something. You can count on Franklin to drop everything and be there in a flash. He always seems to know the right thing to do in any situation and brings a smile and positive attitude with him. If you are sick, he will text or check up on you. Ask him for a favor and he will happily oblige. Franklin is thoughtful, polite, and giving.

However, this isn't simply a one-way relationship, since Franklin needs affirmation, approval, and love in return. He can become demanding and needy when he does not feel validated or appreciated. He can even be mean or aggressive about it. Sometimes boundaries are a problem for Franklin. He can be too intrusive and too nosy which can cause him problems if he is a gossip too.

Case Vignette:

Peggy (point one) has been home from school sick and knows that she will miss a second day of school. She texts Franklin (point two) and asks him to get her the assignments she has missed. In Franklin's attempt to help, he has to track down a couple of Peggy's teachers, which makes him late for class. He becomes so focused on getting Peggy's work that he forgets to write down his own homework assignments.

Wings of Point Two:

As mentioned, the wings are the points that are to either side of each *Teeneatype* point. The wings reflect certain features that make the actual point more inclusive of other qualities.

One Wing:

When Franklin has a one wing, he will share some of Peggy's qualities. He will be more of a perfectionist and be concerned with doing the right thing. He will look to rules for guidance. Giving will be viewed as a form of duty and service.

Three Wing:

With a three wing, Franklin will take on some of the qualities of Trent, who you will meet in the next chapter. He will be a giver who performs at all costs. He will make himself available by "doing it all" to maintain a positive self-image. It is important that Franklin's external image is seen as generous and helpful.

TRENT THE PERFORMER

Point 3

Let's meet Trent.

From the outside:

Trent is the all-American golden boy. His capital T for Trent is associated with words as *task-focused*, *team builder*, *talented*, *time-oriented*, and *tunnel vision*. Trent will most likely be voted the most likely to succeed in his high school class. He is always up to the task and performs as a high achiever.

Trent is close to being a straight A student, star athlete, captain of the football team, and student body president. He is a member of the Rotary club and serves on a number of service boards, both at school and in the community.

Trent has many different roles. He knows how to dress and play the part. He is extremely busy and most of the time doing something productive. Trent has many short- and long-term goals. He is success-oriented and focuses on achieving as much as possible in any given day. His daily and weekly schedules are packed with a variety of constant activities and tasks. Trent has difficulty in knowing what to do with himself when he stops doing and performing.

What is going on inside of Trent?

Trent has lost sight of what is his essential nature and compensates through achievement. Trent's self-image and the image he shows others are of a person who is successful and accomplished. To attain this image, he has learned how to replace feelings with tasks. Trent learned as a child that he could be rewarded for performance and that doing was preferred to expressing his feelings. Because his feelings are continuously pushed aside, an empty space developed inside of Trent, and no matter how much he does or accomplishes, he cannot fill this void.

Because his inner life is focused on goals, success, and performance, he does not value feelings when they come up either in himself or others. He views feelings as inefficient and as obstacles to what he believes he has to do. Trent believes that feelings do not support his image of success, and he has learned to distract himself by constantly performing. Because our American culture supports and represents point three, Trent is rewarded by every aspect of his life in which he is an achiever. It does not appear that Trent has any problems other than being stressed and overworked at times.

MOVEMENT IN THE ENNEAGRAM

In the Enneagram system, you move directly to two other points, in addition to the wings. This can vary from situation to situation. For point three, the movement is to point nine and point six.

When Trent moves to nine:

When Trent moves to nine, he takes on the qualities of the mediator. Here, he is able to expand his tunnel vision to become more aware of the whole picture. Rather than focusing in on one specific task or idea, he can be open to other possibilities.

In nine, Trent can also become a procrastinator and lose his ability to stay focused. Since Trent does not really understand the concept of relaxation, he can also become frustrated in nine because very little gets accomplished. Because nines are able to be quite content in their inertia and internal state of being without a plan or goal, Trent can use this point as a way of learning the benefit of both relaxation and non-activity. If Trent can risk this kind of vulnerability, it is an opportunity for growth. To be without activity puts point three in a position where feelings will surface more readily and the individual can become more honest with him or herself.

When Trent moves to six:

When Trent moves to point six, he begins to doubt himself and can become quite fearful. The term "the imposter syndrome" defines people who, though outwardly successful, feel like they are frauds or fakes at what they are doing regardless of their achievements. When Trent is in six, his doubting mind will take over, making him challenge himself and question his own motives. For someone as image-focused as Trent, this experience can be uncomfortable but can enable him to clarify his priorities and the image he is projecting.

Because Trent does require game plans, strategies, and problem-solving skills to accomplish all his goals, point six offers him additional tools. Sixes are keen detectives and strategists. Trent needs to be careful not to become arrogant in taking an anti-authority position, which sixes thrive on.

Trent and Romantic Relationships:

Trent is attracted to girls who are positive, outgoing, and very active. He has little tolerance for "couch potatoes." Because Trent's image is important to him, he is concerned with how he and a girl appear as a couple. She has to complement his idea of what a couple needs to both look and act like. He tends to define romance in this way: If a girl fits the image he desires, he can create the mood and style required to create and maintain the relationship.

Because Trent has difficulty with his feelings, he has trouble offering emotional support. He tends to be a good problem solver, so he is capable of offering fix-it solutions, but he certainly isn't interested in long conversations, either listening to or tending to a girl's feelings.

Since Trent is extremely busy, he will schedule time with a romantic partner, just as he does all other activities and appointments. It isn't meant to be personal, just practical.

Trent and Friendships:

Trent's friendships are centered on activities. He knows a lot of people with whom he does many different things with. Whether it is sports, schoolwork, student government, clubs, etc., he is a natural at choosing the appropriate role to play and performance to give. Trent does not usually get to know people in a close, personal way because the activity is the basis of the relationship. Trent does not seem to think this is a problem; as long as his friends are available for whatever he is up to, the friendships are treated as golden.

Trent is competitive but fair. He desires success in all areas of his life, including his version of "friendship." He is disappointed when someone cancels on him too often or doesn't play fair, and he tends to avoid such people. Trent has an agenda and isn't patient with or tolerant of what he considers "bad" behavior.

Case Vignette:

Trent (point three) asks Peggy (point one) if she will proofread a speech he is working on for school elections. Peggy agrees and, after reading the speech over, starts to explain grammar rules to him and attempts to give Trent a writing lesson. Trent loses his patience and abruptly says, "Just make the corrections, Peggy, I don't want a lecture." Peggy doesn't understand why Trent is so irritated and leaves with hurt feelings.

Wings of Point Three:

As mentioned, the wings are the points that are to either side of each *Teeneatype* point. The wings reflect certain features that make the actual point more inclusive of other qualities.

Two Wing:

When Trent has a two wing, he is a doer who will attempt to be helpful and use performance to gain approval. Like Franklin, he is extroverted and cheerful. He will focus on others with a positive outlook to enhance his self-image.

Four Wing:

When Trent has a four wing, like Maria, whom we will meet in the next chapter, he is more self-absorbed and introspective. He is more in touch with his feelings and understands sadness and melancholy. He is more sensitive and will take some time to figure himself out.

Maria the Tragic-Romantic

Point 4

Let's meet Maria.

From the outside:

Maria is truly unique. We can associate her capital M for Maria with words such as *melancholic, mysterious, moody, melodramatic*, and *multi-dimensional*. When people see Maria, they are not sure what to make of her. She is intense and can be dramatic with a creative, artistic flair, which people are often drawn to. However, because Maria can also be aloof and self-absorbed, it can be difficult to want to be around her for any length of time.

Maria is verbal and self-expressive. She is also articulate and introspective, so it is both natural and easy for her to talk about her feelings. She is always looking for that deeper connection with others. Because her emotional life is extreme, she is often seen as moody. There is a sense that life is like a stage for Maria and that she has created a personal, unique style and set of mannerisms to play out her drama.

What is going on inside of Maria?

It is hard for Maria to experience equanimity in her life because she believes something is missing that others seem to have. This can best be described as envy. Regardless of what Maria has, she comes up lacking in her own eyes and experiences herself as deficient. Maria believes that others are happier, prettier, smarter, more fun, etc. Maria also experiences a built-in sense of abandonment and feelings of rejection and unworthiness. Because attention moves to what is missing, there is a constant need to search for one's purpose or meaning in life. Also, Maria gets stuck thinking the "grass is greener" elsewhere. The restlessness, suffering, and emotional swings are all part of the drama. Maria seeks authenticity; her inner life demands an ongoing search for what is true for her.

MOVEMENT IN THE ENNEAGRAM

In the Enneagram system, you move directly to two other points, in addition to the wings. This can vary from situation to situation. For point four, the movement is to point one and point two.

When Maria moves to two:

When Maria moves to point two, she tends to seek approval from others. Here, her authenticity might be compromised. She might flatter, flirt, and manipulate to get her way. At times she can become a martyr, claiming all that you owe her because of all that she has sacrificed and done for you.

Because point two is the point of the codependent, Maria is also capable of handling a crisis on the spot. She has the ability to shift her attention from self-absorption to concern for someone else's well-being. At those moments, Maria's focus shifts to outside and away from herself. In doing this, she becomes accommodating and adaptable.

When Maria moves to one:

When Maria moves to point one, she is face-to-face with her "overidealized" view of how she and her world should be. This is the place where she strives for the unobtainable. Maria reflects on the airbrushed, perfect image of herself, the fantasy of "the rich and famous" lifestyle, the perfect family, etc. This is the place her dreamer self strives toward, but she is never able to meet the ideals that she has created for herself.

If Maria is able to become more realistic both with herself and others in point one, she can use it as an opportunity to move beyond self-criticism and judgment. She can access a sense of correctness and become responsible. If Maria allows herself, she can set manageable goals, create a plan, and establish a routine and structure that will serve her.

Maria and Romantic Relationships:

Relationships are difficult for Maria. Because attention always goes to what is missing, there is a push-pull pattern built into the romance. If the boy crush calls too often, Maria thinks he is needy and is turned off. If he doesn't call her often enough, she thinks he isn't interested and questions herself.

Dating and even hanging out can be painful for Maria. If the boy crush doesn't offer adequate attention, there can be an upset. Maria is very sensitive and aware of her own thoughts and feelings. She also assumes that she is attuned to the boy's thoughts and feelings. Because of her feelings of unworthiness and abandonment, she will create a drama that tests the romance and inevitably makes the abandonment real. Repeatedly, Maria ends up alone.

Maria and Friendships

Friendships move through cycles for Maria. There is the early period of "falling in love" with people and placing them on pedestals. Like a new romance, the beginning phase is wonderful. As time goes on, however, enchantment diminishes as a sense of ordinariness sets in. But if a drama ensues and the relationship is threatened, the person becomes more attractive and interesting.

Maria can be a very sensitive and caring friend. Because she is so introspective, she can offer valuable and helpful support and insight to friends. When her moodiness is regulated, she is much easier to be with. Since her curiosity feeds her creative and imaginative side, there is usually something interesting that Maria has to share.

Case Vignette:

Maria (point four) has a crush on Conrad (point eight) and asks Franklin (point two) to introduce her to him. Finally, Franklin arranges a meeting and Conrad asks Maria to go to the football game that coming Friday. At first, Maria is very excited and plans what outfit to wear and imagines how the evening will go. As Friday gets closer, she begins to wonder if she even wants to go.

Wings of Point Four:

As mentioned, the wings are the points that are to either side of each Teeneatype point. The wings reflect certain features that make the actual point more inclusive of other qualities.

Three Wing:

Maria with a three wing will share some of Trent's traits. She will usually be more dramatic and performance-focused. Maria uses activity and image to express her need for uniqueness. She will be more extroverted and outgoing with a creative flair.

Five Wing:

Maria with a five wing is more introverted and quiet. She will be more cerebral and less a performer. Often she will enjoy solitary, introspective time dedicated to more mental activities, such as reading and writing. She is more reserved and self-contained.

MARK THE OBSERVER

Point 5

Let's meet Mark.

From the outside:

Mark can appear to be shy and quiet. In fact, he is *mindful, mental, masterful, miserly,* and a *minimalist.* Mark is preoccupied with a lot of intellectual concerns and challenges, so he usually has a lot on his mind. He is interested in things that require analysis and strategic thinking. Mark is also a keen observer. This combination of solid mental abilities and observation skills makes him a natural detective and researcher.

Mark likes thinking and pondering ideas and like Trent (point 3), doesn't get caught up in feelings, which seem irrational and illogical. Mark likes to be frugal and sometimes is accused of being cheap. He tends to minimize his needs and understands his frugality as being economical and reasonable. As a five, Mark's logo could read "Less is more." But this motto would not apply to Mark's search for knowledge. In this area, Mark can become insatiable and will absorb reams of data and information.

Because Mark is an observer by nature, he is busy focused on others rather than thinking about himself. His lack of insight (sight inward) tends to make him both unaware and detached from his needs. Mark struggles with being dependent, so he does not easily reach out and ask others to meet his needs. Since Mark's interests are focused more on objects and ideas rather than people, he often isn't aware that he is missing out on people contact for long periods. Mark stimulates his own mind, and that is often the only connection he believes he needs.

What is going on inside of Mark?

Mark has come to replace the full experience of "living life" by experiencing his life through his intellect. By "living in his head," he can protect himself from experiencing his feelings, though not a conscious decision. His avarice (greed) has replaced nonattachment. By downsizing and minimizing his needs, Mark avoids depending on or reaching out to others. This creates detachment. Nonattachment is actually the opposite. It is the ability to connect, have a full experience, and then step back.

Mark also manages his need for privacy by staying extremely compartmentalized. Mark only shares selective parts of himself with select individuals. Privacy is a means of protection and control. Because Mark has difficulty accessing feelings, his identity is based on an intellectual understanding of himself. He can even seem mechanical and robot-like in his responses, devoid of any expression of feelings. Mark uses mental observation rather than emotional connection when he interacts with others. He views the world as through a camera lens. Sometimes it is painful for Mark to be more of an observer than a participant in his own life.

Movement in the Enneagram

In the Enneagram system you move directly to two other points, in addition to the wings. This can vary from situation to situation. For point five, the movement is to point seven and point eight.

When Mark moves to seven:

When Mark moves to seven, he becomes more relaxed both in his pleasures and interests. Additionally, he is able to synthesize his knowledge (i.e., take a variety of ideas and even if they are unrelated, put them all together). Mark likes using a system for things, and in seven, he can go far beyond just analyzing things, almost like taking individual blocks and putting them together to form a workable pattern. Here, he often takes unrelated material and puts it together to create fresh and original ideas.

In seven, Mark can be charming and witty. It is a safe place for him to interact because feelings are also not part of the seven's persona. In seven, Mark has fun planning and coming up with multiple options for many projects and hobbies. The problem that can arise is Mark ending up juggling too many things because he has overcommitted. He also can tend to back-burner things and deadlines can be difficult to meet.

When Mark moves to eight:

When Mark moves to eight, he can show a "big" reaction, namely anger and aggression. Because Mark is typically contained and exercises self-restraint, these reactions hit like sudden jolts. Mark doesn't like to get angry or show emotion, so it takes "big" energy in order for it to occur. Afterward, Mark is usually emotionally spent.

Mark can also be a "big" protector in eight. He stands up for what he believes in. Relationships can be complicated for Mark because people are often emotionally draining and demanding. When he is in eight, he's better able to deal with others' expectations of him.

Mark and Romantic Relationships

A romantic relationship can awaken and boost an experience of feeling alive in Mark, however difficult and uncomfortable this might be at first. Mark is fearful of intimacy and closeness, so there is tremendous awkwardness in figuring out the best ways to make a connection. If Mark finds a girl with whom he can discuss intellectual ideas, he will be more comfortable. Something like mental ping-pong is a good strategy for flirting.

Technology, especially texting, makes it so much easier for Mark to communicate; he can think and type, rather than have a live conversation. Mark also likes to take things very, very slowly and is not in a rush to get into a relationship. He won't figure out his feelings for some time, although he does review them after the date, when he is alone and safe in the privacy of his own space.

Mark always holds back some part of himself. He can be generous in some areas but will not fully share himself in terms of time, money, affection, feelings, knowledge, etc.

Mark and Friendships:

Mark is easily distracted and preoccupied with his intellectual curiosity. Although he enjoys his solitude, he can get lonely if he isolates himself too much. Mark likes to spend time with friends who share his intellectual interests and activities. If he is playing a game, such as tennis or soccer, he likes to discuss and analyze the game, the players, the strategies, etc. He enjoys people who share his pursuits. But even if you don't share his interests, that is okay with Mark, as long as you listen to his thoughts and ideas. Mark's friends complement different aspects of him. If all of Mark's friends were put together in one place, they would probably not know each other. They represent different parts of Mark's life, and because of his need for privacy and habit of compartmentalizing, they might also never meet unless Mark has an event that brought them all together.

Case Vignette:

Mark (point five) wants to start a science club at school. About ten students show up, thinking it might be fun to do science experiments and invent things. Mark presents an outline to the group that includes books to read, research ideas, and field work. Most of the students get up and walk out of the classroom. Mark shrugs and says to Peggy (point one), "I don't understand. The work is so interesting and fun!"

Wings of Point Five:

As mentioned, the wings are the points that are to either side of each *Teeneatype* point. The wings reflect certain features that make the actual point more inclusive of other qualities.

Four Wing:

If Mark has a four wing, he will take on some traits similar to Maria. He will tend to be more introspective and more connected to his feelings. He can become melancholy and have a sense of longing. He will be more sensitive but not always equipped to manage his feelings.

Six Wing:

Mark with a six wing will be more like Paul, who we will meet in the next chapter, detached and cautious. He will tend to be preoccupied with disruptive thoughts and an active imagination. He will usually be fearful, loyal, and reserved with a six wing.

Paul and Rusty the Troopers

Point 6

Let's meet Paul and Rusty.

From the outside:

Because point six is represented by two very different personality types, we get to meet both Paul and Rusty. Paul is a phobic (fearful) six, and Rusty is what is called a counter-phobic six (challenges fear). Paul is *phobic*, *paranoid*, *panicky*, *passive*, and *procrastinates*. In contrast, Rusty is *rebellious*, *rough*, *resistant*, and a *risk taker*.

Paul and Rusty have issues with emotional security and a basic fear of abandonment. They respect authority because they have a need to be protected but will challenge authority because they lack the trust that others will be there for them.

Paul will usually be the loyalist; he follows the rules and listens to authority. However, at times he will test those in authority in order to determine if he can truly count on them. Rusty, on the other hand, has no problem outwardly challenging the rules, often pushing through his fear. Rusty can look a lot like Conrad, the eight, but each is motivated for different reasons.

When Rusty is showing his anti-authority bravado, he is testing the waters, scanning for danger and threat. Conrad, the eight, on the other hand, is asserting command, taking leadership in a situation. Paul and Rusty are also excellent observers, like Mark at point five. Because they scan the environment for danger and threats, they too would make good detectives and investigators.

What is going on inside of Paul and Rusty?

Paul and Rusty have both lost sight of courage because of their emotional insecurity and have replaced it with fear. This fear becomes the motive to constantly seek out the courage to manage their distrust of the world. Because Paul and Rusty cannot trust, they are filled with doubt, often to the point of having difficulty making up their minds about the simplest things. Paul can be so indecisive that he will often change his mind over and over and then be unable to follow through on his initial intention. Rusty, on the other hand, often pushes through his indecision by making impulsive, reckless choices.

Paul's constant self-checking and Rusty's dare-devil attitude can create problems for each of them. Paul is never able to accomplish as much as he wants to because he is so fickle he can't commit to completing things. Rusty is impatient and hasty, often rushing through life with little attention to the consequences of his actions.

Paul and Rusty constantly live with a high level of anxiety but deal with it differently. Paul tries to not make waves and avoids conflict in an attempt to find security and safety. Rusty uses the anxiety to fuel his adrenaline so that he can push through the demands of the environment.

MOVEMENT IN THE ENNEAGRAM

In the Enneagram system, you move directly to two other points, in addition to the wings. This can vary from situation to situation. For point six, the movement is to point three and point nine.

When Paul and Rusty move to three:

When Paul and Rusty move to point three, they become task-focused. This is very difficult for both of them because their fear creates a stop-start pattern of movement. Both Paul and Rusty need to relax to some degree in order to make any progress in performance. Paul is more aware of the inner tape playing in his head that makes him doubt himself. This, in turn, causes him to be distracted and again frightened.

If Rusty can stay focused on the task, then something can be accomplished. Otherwise, he will lose his edge and the movement will become like running in circles.

When Paul and Rusty move to nine:

In nine, both Paul and Rusty are able to relax. Because the move to nine is a shift from their heads to their bodies, they can temporarily get rid of their fear. Both can also experience a sense of spaciness, like nines, and can feel as if they have lost their motivation.

In nine, both Paul and Rusty are more secure in their ability to see the bigger picture, connect to others, and notice people's positive qualities. In nine, Paul and Rusty are affected by their body sensations and emotions. This moves them out of their head and into their bodies, away from fear and doubt.

Paul and Rusty and Romantic Relationships:

Paul and Rusty are quite different in their pursuit of romance. Paul might attempt to warm up to a girl but will be tentative and uncomfortable in his behavior. Because doubt surfaces constantly, he simply feels insecure and awkward. It will take some time for him to establish a trustworthy connection.

Rusty is bold, even abrupt at times, in his approach. He will mask his fear by being smooth and calculated. He might act cocky and be a show-off. He will probably drive too fast to impress a girl and might even try to put a girl on the back of a motorcycle.

Both Paul and Rusty go through a lengthy period of testing the girls they date. They both want to understand their motives and intentions. Always preparing for the worst, they have trouble feeling safe. Paul might be sporadic and inconsistent in his availability to you at the beginning of a dating relationship. Rusty is somewhat different and can come on more strongly and seem very available then suddenly disappear. Don't try to figure out their patterns. They both need time to figure out their own minds and where they stand with the girl.

Paul and Rusty and Friendships:

Both Paul and Rusty are extremely loyal to their friends. Once you are perceived as trustworthy, Paul and Rusty will be devoted and loyal to you for life. As with romantic relationships, friendships will go through a testing phase before Paul and Rusty are convinced you are true blue.

Sixes are allies to the weak, the underdogs in life. Paul's heart might go out to you, but Rusty will "go to bat for you." If a bully is bothering you, he won't think twice about beating him up. Paul will tend to be interested in tamer activities, such as chess, video games, and nonaggressive sports. If you want a run for your money and like car racing, skydiving, and aggressive contact sports, Rusty is your man.

Case Vignette:

Rusty (point six) and Paul (point six) have trouble getting along. They like each other but don't understand each other much of the time. They decide to try to go out on a double date. Rusty wants to do something fun and exciting, like go to an amusement park or go roller skating. Paul just wants to go to a movie or out to dinner.

Rusty says, "Come on, Paul, stop being such a deadbeat."

Paul is offended and states, "Whatever you suggest isn't safe. I'm just not a risk taker."

Wings of Point Six:

As mentioned, the wings are the points that are to either side of each *Teeneatype* point. The wings reflect certain features that make the actual point more inclusive of other qualities.

Five Wing:

When Paul or Rusty has a five wing, they will be more introverted and reserved, like Mark. Because they both are uncertain of others' motives, they are usually trying to second-guess others using keen observation skills. Both can be serious and will tend to withdraw when uncomfortable or fearful.

Seven Wing:

When Paul or Rusty has a seven wing, they will tend to be lighter and more relaxed, like Penny, whom you will meet in the next chapter. They will be able to find the positive and good in life in spite of all their doubts and fears. Both will tend to hold forth and be imaginative storytellers as a way to manage their uncertainty.

Penny the Optimist

Point 7

Let's meet Penny.

From the outside:

Penny is popular! Her capital P stands for *positive*, *pleasure seeker*, *planner*, *partier*, and a puella (*forever young*). Penny loves to have a good time and is the eternal optimist. She is upbeat and is able to turn anything that others would see as a downer into something positive.

Penny turns lemons into lemonade. She is at her best when she is able to juggle all the many parts of her life successfully. Penny likes to follow the fun, and because she is so enthusiastic and positive, others are readily attracted to her personality and lighthearted nature.

Penny lives in her head and, as a mental type, is often fascinated with new and interesting ideas and experiences. She is eager to have new adventures and is spontaneous in whatever piques her interest. Because her habit is to generate multiple options, there is always too much to do. So some things get placed on the back burner. Penny is also easily distracted by what catches her attention in the moment. Penny fuels new heights of arousal by keeping a lot of stimulation and activity going on. If outside stimulation ever fails, Penny keeps her own high-spirited self going by pumping herself up from the inside.

What is going on inside of Penny?

Because Penny has come to mask fear by using gluttony to satisfy her insatiable appetite, be it food, entertainment, or experiences, she has lost sight of her essence, which is called sobriety. Sobriety gives Penny a more "sober" and serious view of life, which enables her to embrace both the positive and negative sides of a situation.

To stay focused on things that are unpleasant is difficult for Penny, so she will do almost anything to avoid pain. Her primary strategy is her "monkey mind" by which she will fixate her attention on one specific thing and then quickly shift attention to something else and then something else, etc.

This rapid shift of attention enables Penny to stay spontaneous and present; however, she can also walk away in an instant from things that become disinteresting or difficult. Penny rationalizes her thoughts and behaviors by living according to the motto, "Life is too short to spoil it with being unhappy." It is easy not to suffer when every unhappy thing is avoided or replaced with something pleasant.

Penny dislikes being roped into or committed to anything. Planning is fine as long as there is a way out of the commitment. To be happy is to have choices, and to have choices is to keep the door open, leave room for change, and "go with the flow."

MOVEMENT IN THE ENNEAGRAM

In the Enneagram system, you move directly to two other points, in addition to the wings. This can vary from situation to situation. For point seven, the movement is to point one and point five.

When Penny moves to one:

When Penny moves to point one, she becomes more focused and single-minded in her outlook. She will usually get a job perfected and completed in point one. The positive aspect of this position allows Penny to hold to an ethical code and honor her commitments. She will be more responsible and accountable in one.

The downside of this position is a result of Penny's gluttony. She does not like to feel deprived. She can, therefore, take on a position of entitlement. Point one is about the "shoulds" and judgments, but Penny is not as much concerned about the right and wrong of a situation as she is about getting her fair share of pleasure from it.

When Penny moves to five:

When Penny moves to point five, it is because she has a need to detach from too much stimulation and will retreat inside herself. Penny can then get quieter and observe her options from a more objective position. When she is less stimulated, her brain slows down and she becomes more introspective and might even become aware of her fears, pain, and feelings of inferiority. However, this won't usually last for too long, since pain and depression are avoided at all costs.

Because Penny is calmer, even constricted and restrained in five, she can develop a clear strategy and a "forced choice" from this position. Without external pressure, and from a place of retreat and solitude, it is easier for Penny to make up her mind and figure out her priorities. However, this is, at best, difficult, given the endless possibilities and choices life has to offer.

Penny and Romantic Relationships:

Romance is fun for Penny because she makes it "all about her." She can be an upbeat, adventurous, and playful girlfriend. It is important to understand that Penny is self-centered, but this is not an indication of how much she might care for you. Penny is interested in keeping the relationship positive and fun. She is open to talking about most topics as long as the conversation stays upbeat. Negativity is a big turn off for Penny. She likes to keep her interaction light and chatty. Her broad happy smile and charm brings much joy and laughter to the relationship.

Most any activity can be a good time for Penny. She is easily entertained and easily entertaining. Because of her high energy and enthusiasm, she can easily "burn the candle at both ends" as long as there is enough fun and pleasure in the mix. Penny can tolerate commitment if she has sufficient freedom and independence. When too many demands are placed on her and she feels pressured, she will flee and often for good.

Penny and Friendships:

Penny is popular with most everyone. She hangs out with her closest friends but is welcome and included wherever she goes. She knows a lot of people, and her optimism and warmth make her very likeable. Penny is friendly and outgoing, so she easily reaches out to others, and they are readily attracted to her. Penny is free-spirited and usually can be spontaneous in following her joys and pleasures. She is always ready to try something new and the first to sign up for an adventure. She also has a tendency to switch plans at the last minute in order to do something she thinks would be more fun and enjoyable. Her friends sometimes find this annoying.

Penny is the one her friends turn to when they are in a funk and want to feel better. She can always find the silver lining in every sad story. Because Penny avoids her own pain and unhappiness, she puts most of her energy into ways to self-soothe. Consequently, she has a good supply of helpful hints to make others feel better.

Case Vignette:

Penny (point seven) and Mark (point five) decide to team up for a history assignment that involves an oral presentation. They divide up the work, and Penny keeps insisting that it needs to be fun. Because Penny likes to keep her options open, she has no problem planning little skits that she and Mark can do together. Mark begins to worry if Penny is getting any of the assignment down on paper.

The night before, Mark texts Penny, "Are you almost done?"

Penny texts back, "I'm almost there. I haven't quite started, but I have all night."

Wings of Point Seven:

As mentioned, the wings are the points that are to either side of each *Teeneatype* point. The wings reflect certain features that make the actual point more inclusive of other qualities.

Eight Wing:

If Penny has an eight wing, she can be bossy and aggressive, like Conrad, whom we'll meet in the next chapter. She also can be boastful and loud. Penny knows how to be the life of the party and easily overdoes it.

Six Wing:

With a six wing, Penny will share some of Paul's and Rusty's traits. She can be witty but also question things. She will tend to be highly imaginative and a good planner with a lot of creative intelligence.

CONRAD THE CHALLENGER

Point 8

Let's Meet Conrad.

From the outside:

Conrad announces himself as he enters any room or situation. The C for Conrad stands for *competitive, combative, candid, controlling,* and *charismatic.* Conrad likes contact and respects anyone who stands up to him. He is at his best as a protector and when he is on the lookout for the weak and the helpless who needs his care. As much as he is seen to muscle up and take on anyone who dares to challenge him, he will go to great lengths to save a stranded animal or help a driver in a stalled car.

Conrad goes after life with great gusto. He lusts after things and experiences and feeds his big appetite with everything that interests him. Because of his tendency to be impulsive and to indulge in excess, he pushes boundaries at all costs. Conrad is also very volatile and has to monitor his anger, or he can easily become aggressive and explosive.

Conrad is grandiose and sees himself as "larger than life." This enables him to see himself as unstoppable and to believe he can accomplish or acquire anything he desires and sets his mind to. Conrad pushes hard and never gives up. He operates with an angel on one shoulder and a devil on the other. Some of his oppositional behavior exists because he is trying to figure out what he wants. He often determines his own position in the process of challenging something or someone else.

What is going on inside of Conrad?

Conrad's search for truth motivates him to control people and situations. He assumes that he is the enforcer of both justice and fairness. In Conrad's mind, innocence has become equivalent to weakness and has to be defended against. Conrad's enormous desire and energy to satisfy his needs is referred to as lust. The problem Conrad faces is that he is unclear about his needs, and he uses his reactivity in order to figure them out.

When Conrad is in challenger mode, he is invincible and unstoppable. He will break rules and push limits and boundaries at all costs. Rules apply to others but don't necessarily apply to him.

Conrad's impulsive bull-headed style leaves him unaware of the impact he can actually have on others. Unfortunately, his tendency to deny his own personal weaknesses and to see things only from his own point of view fuels his confrontational style. It is difficult for Conrad to see how he provokes and offends others. He defends his position by stating that he acts on behalf of justice (e.g., "I wouldn't have had to hurt you if you had listened to me.").

MOVEMENT IN THE ENNEAGRAM

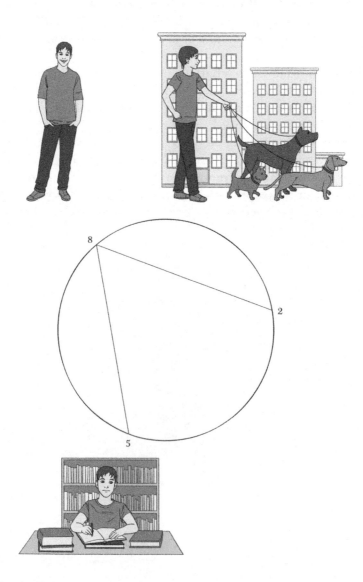

In the Enneagram system, you move directly to two other points, in addition to the wings. This can vary from situation to situation. For point eight, the movement is to point five and point two.

When Conrad moves to five:

When Conrad moves to point five, he becomes withdrawn and quiet. He seeks privacy and actually can become introspective which he can't do in point eight. Conrad can gain some self-awareness in five and a better understanding of his actions. Here is an opportunity for him to overcome his black-and-white style of thinking. In five, Conrad can become compartmentalized, which enables him to pay attention more selectively and be less overwhelmed by the world at large. He can become extremely focused and spend long periods on mental activities.

Withdrawal and isolation can have a less positive aspect for Conrad; he can simply use this position to tune out. He might, thereby, reduce his stress, but nothing is really learned. Additionally, Conrad can use this mental stance as a convenient means to rationalize his actions and distance from any feelings.

When Conrad moves to two:

When Conrad moves to point two, he allows himself to relax and become more of a giver. In this position, he usually can be more vulnerable and emotionally softer. Conrad appreciates this position, particularly when it feels like it is in accord with his truth. He can let go of his anger and his need for control.

In the giving mode, Conrad is able to experience his own sensitivity and can be more sensitive to the needs of others. He will be generous with his time, energy, and personal possessions. On a less positive note, in two, he can use giving as a form of manipulation and as a means of satisfying his personal agenda. He can also become increasingly demanding and needy in two or see himself as a martyr. In the martyr position, Conrad might think "everyone only calls me when they need something from me."

Conrad and Romantic Relationships:

Conrad tends to be direct and forthcoming. He prefers girls who are independent and strong. His imposing, intense energy can be intimidating. Because Conrad requires a lot of personal freedom, he refuses to be controlled and told what to do.

Conrad can be generous with his time and often parties into the wee hours. He craves fun, excitement, and high levels of stimulation. Conrad is prone to excess, and is always pushing for things and testing limits. Therefore, a romantic relationship with Conrad will require dealing with confrontation since he provokes arguments as a form of contact. "How much do you really care?" "Are you strong enough to hang in?" Being with Conrad is somewhat like being on a roller coaster without good traction. It is a very bumpy ride but usually exciting and unpredictable.

Conrad has trouble showing softer feelings and dependency needs. He masks this by either distancing and withdrawing or compensating by taking over and being a girl's protector and adviser. Conrad is extremely sensitive, truth be told, but will not usually show it. He likes his partners to be honest and direct; he is not a game player.

Conrad and Friendships:

Conrad is popular. He has your back if he thinks you are being mistreated. However, when Conrad gets out of line, he himself can be a big bully.

Conrad is always willing to pitch in and help out a friend. He is interested in contact, so he also tends to have a large network of people he is connected to. Conrad likes to see himself as generous and helpful and will encourage his friends to count on him. However, when they do, he can feel taken for granted and underappreciated. He usually isn't aware that it was he who insisted on their asking for his help.

Conrad needs physical outlets to release pent-up energy and anger. He loves to play competitive, contact sports. When he is with friends, it is important for him to have stimulating activities and conversation.

Conrad is confrontational, and his anger can easily flare. He at times gets himself into trouble, thinking he is defending justice, but actually seen by others as hot-tempered and looking for a fight. It's a bit of a double bind trying to reason with Conrad when all he thinks he is doing is being a "protector of the truth."

Case Vignette:

Conrad's (point eight) campaign for school president against Trent (point three) is not going well. *I have to win hands down!* Conrad thinks.

The week before, Conrad overhears a secret about Trent that he knows, if it gets around, will assure him a solid victory. Conrad also knows that Franklin's (point two) reputation borders on being "the gossip boy." He will leak the secret about Trent's DUI from the summer to Franklin, and the election will sure to be his. Conrad justifies his behavior by thinking, *Everyone has a right to know the truth about Trent. He did it to himself.*

Wings of Point Eight:

As mentioned, the wings are the points that are to either side of each *Teeneatype* point. The wings reflect certain features that make the actual point more inclusive of other qualities.

Seven Wing:

If Conrad has a seven wing, like Penny, he will be bold, fun, and impulsive. He will tend to be more extroverted with high energy and a positive outlook. He can easily be distracted.

Nine Wing:

If Conrad has a nine wing, he will be more mellow and relaxed like Sarah, whom we will meet in the next chapter. Although less confrontational, he can become very headstrong and oppositional. He will tend to be less energetic and easily neglect his needs. Similar to Sarah, "he forgets himself."

SARAH THE MEDIATOR

Point 9

Let's meet Sarah.

From the outside:

Sarah appears mellow, a go-with-the-flow kind of girl. Sarah's capital "S" is about being *selfless*, *self-forgetting*, *sacrificial*, *stubborn*, and *self-effacing*. Sarah doesn't know herself, nor does she even recognize the importance of figuring out her identity. Sarah is mostly focused on mediating and tending to everyone else's needs. She actually appears content doing very little with her life.

Sarah's motivation to get things done only evolves after much avoidance and procrastinating. She is actually motivated to avoid action, to not make waves. She isn't aware that she doesn't know her needs; therefore, nothing matters that much, except for keeping the peace and staying comfortable. Sarah's inertia and ability to remain at rest enable her to be the classic "couch potato," who loses herself in television and video games for hours. Nonessential tasks easily replace important things. Homework and chores are easily forgotten, and time is readily wasted.

Although Sarah has issues with anger, she avoids them by staying away from conflicts and confrontations to the best of her ability. Sarah also has difficulty making decisions because she sees the value of all points of view. So to commit to one position is very difficult, particularly because she doesn't identify her own point of view. All of Sarah's wavering and inability to assert herself makes her passive-aggressive. Sarah struggles remembering herself, so she will tend to go along with others rather than figure herself out.

What is going on inside of Sarah?

Sarah's slothful tendencies of idleness and self-neglect have replaced the virtue of right action. Sarah's inner dial has been turned way down, so the questions "Who am I?" "What are my needs?" and "What are my goals?" have been long overlooked and forgotten. Instead, Sarah has learned to focus on the needs of others. Her own self-focus has become replaced by other people's requirements and demands of her. Through her childhood, this habit became so ingrained that she lost sight of her own self.

Sarah pays attention to many things at the same time. Her multitrack thinking makes her appear spacey at times because she is shifting her attention from one inner thought to another, even as she is engaged in conversation. She can do this because she leaves her own self out of the equation. Sarah is open-minded and nonjudgmental compared with her point one neighbor Peggy. She is also nonconfrontational in contrast to her point eight neighbor, Conrad, the challenger.

Sarah is the diplomat and can see everyone else's blind spot. Sarah has no distortion in her own lens, so she sees everyone else clearly. She just can't see herself. Sarah can be a hard worker as a result of doing what is expected of her, rather than as a result of being self-motivated. Sarah wants everyone happy and content which will ensure peaceful coexistence.

MOVEMENT IN THE ENNEAGRAM

In the Enneagram system, you move directly to two other points, in addition to the wings. This can vary from situation to situation. For point nine, the movement is to point six and point three.

When Sarah moves to six:

When Sarah moves to point six, she can become fearful and worried. Because this is a mental point, she can end up ruminating and worrying but not necessarily doing anything about it. In six, if Sarah becomes too frightened, she can be paralyzed by her fear and withdraw completely.

The more positive aspect of six emerges when Sarah can become vigilant and figure out a plan to manage an obstacle. If she can use logic and strategic thinking, she can avoid getting stuck. In six, Sarah also develops her loyalties and can create allies. From this perspective, she can better understand the motives of others and create more realistic expectations.

When Sarah moves to three:

When Sarah is in three, she is able to perform and stay in task mode. It is very important for Sarah to be aware of how much of her action is based on her own agenda and how much is based on someone else's. Too often Sarah gives herself away. If she is in touch with her own personal goals, she will be able to stay focused, like a three, and be oriented toward achievement, recognition, and acceptance.

If Sarah is operating under someone else's authority, she will be action-oriented only to the extent that her "boss" keeps the pressure on her and pushes her with deadlines and work output requirements.

Sarah needs to find the motivation and meaning of her actions within herself, or she and everyone around her will be continually frustrated by her inconsistent performance.

Sarah and Romantic Relationships:

Sarah tends to lose herself in romantic relationships. Because of her tendency to merge, she will easily take on the beloved's agenda and simply attach herself to whatever is being offered. It is hard for Sarah to hold on to any part of her personal identity when she is in a relationship because she automatically accommodates the partner and is molded by the partner's needs and requirements.

Sarah's partner might in time get frustrated, since Sarah has trouble making decisions, whether it is choosing a restaurant, movie, or place and time to get together. Although her go-with-the-flow style might be appreciated in the beginning, it can become tiresome for her partner to have to make all the plans.

Sarah also avoids conflict so that she can avoid her anger. Because of her degree of avoidance, she doesn't deal directly with what is bothering her. Over time, this can cause stress on the relationship, since it is hard to figure Sarah out. It is a challenge to get Sarah to talk about anything that makes her uncomfortable. Otherwise, Sarah is agreeable, comfortable to be with, and usually adapts to most anything.

Sarah and Friendships:

Sarah is easy to get along with and is, therefore, well liked. Because she is not much of an initiator, she does not usually approach and invite her friends to do things. It's not because she isn't interested; it just doesn't occur to her to reach out and be proactive. Sarah is usually available when friends invite her to do things. Sometimes she has to say no because she is often behind getting her homework done. Her dawdling and self-forgetting can get in the way.

Sarah does better with friends who are active and involved and will encourage her to participate in activities. Since she gets distracted easily and wastes time, it helps Sarah to have a friend keep track of the times and locations of events.

When someone needs a comfortable easy buddy to hang out with, Sarah is a handy friend to have. Just don't plan to leave the driving up to Sarah!

Case vignette:

Sarah (point nine) takes music lessons with Paul (point six). They are preparing a piece for a recital together. Sarah has trouble making it to practice sessions with Paul. She is always so apologetic it is hard for Paul to get mad at her. As the recital date approaches, Paul is increasingly anxious and Sarah is increasingly forgetful. When Sarah shows up thirty minutes late for the last practice, Paul explodes. Sarah burst into tears and has no idea why Paul is angry at her.

Wings of Point Nine:

As mentioned, the wings are the points that are to either side of each *Teeneatype* point. The wings reflect certain features that make the actual point more inclusive of other qualities.

One Wing:

If Sarah has a one wing, she will tend to take on some of the qualities of her neighbor Peggy. She will be more of a perfectionist, more organized, and more critical. Sarah will tend to follow the rules and the "shoulds." She will use self-restraint in expressing her anger.

Eight Wing:

If Sarah has an eight wing, she will take on some of Conrad's qualities. She will find it easier to assert herself and express her anger, and she might be more controlling and confrontational. An eight wing will help her speak up and be more direct and honest.

CONCLUSION

By now, I hope you have come to identify with one of the *Teeneatypes*. If you are still uncertain, you can at least eliminate the types that don't resemble you at all. The ones that you identify with mostly, you can try and see if they fit one at a time. It takes practice to develop a keen inner observer. There are additionally adult tests online that you can take to help pinpoint your type. Look up "Enneagram" on the Internet and you will discover many different tests you can self-administer and score.

As I stated at the beginning of this book, my primary goal is to offer you a basic introduction to a psychological system that offers some powerful self-help tools. The *Teeneagram*, based on the Enneagram, offers you insight as to how your attention is organized and gives you the opportunity to understand others as they are to themselves. In time, you will discover how accurate the movement in the system is and how strongly the habits of our type influence all areas of our life.

Anytime that we can learn and observe ourselves, we are opening a new door. Each doorway can lead to knowledge and self-understanding. As we grow, we can develop more self-awareness and learn how to transform ourselves. It all starts with self-observation. Self-discovery is a process that will enrich and add meaning to your life. What you do with it is up to you. My hope is that you make the most of your gifts and that the *Teeneagram* offers you a source of enrichment and self- knowledge.

SUMMARY FOR TEENEAGRAM

Teeneagram: Identity Search Made Easy is an introductory book to the Enneagram. Written for teens and young adults, *Teeneagram* describes a psychological system based on nine different points of view. In the book, nine different characters are portrayed to illustrate the various personality styles and describe how each character's attention is constructed and expressed. *Teeneagram* will help one better understand him/herself, the decisions one makes, the relationships one chooses, and why. One will become aware of how his/her habits, attitudes, and thinking are organized following a very specific pattern as one moves through understanding the influences of one's type. Since there are nine character types, one will discover why his/her behavior, thoughts, and feelings are also experienced by others of the same type. *Teeneagram* is an essential tool to help unlock the inner workings of one's identity and to offer one a road map to develop self-awareness and understand other people in one's life.